Jean-Côme Noguès

# House
## for a
# Mouse

## Illustrated by Anne Velghe

Translated by J. Alison James

**North-South Books / New York / London**

Little Mouse was born in a barn and grew up happily on the farm. One day, her mother said to her: "Now that you're a big girl, it's time for you to set off on your own. You need to find yourself a new home."

A new home—that meant Little Mouse would have to go on an adventure.

She decided that she would like a house with a lot of sun, very little rain, and no cats at all.

Her mother gave her a piece of wheat for her breakfast. Then she kissed Little Mouse good-bye and wished her good luck.

Houses +
Homes

For Mirko, my little boy —A.V.

Copyright © 2005 by NordSüd Verlag AG, Gossau Zürich, Switzerland
First published in Switzerland under the title *Ein eigenes Haus für Tom*
English translation copyright © 2005 by North-South Books Inc., New York

First published in the United States, Great Britain, Canada, Australia, and New Zealand in 2005
by North-South Books, an imprint of NordSüd Verlag AG, Gossau Zürich, Switzerland.
Distributed in the United States by North-South Books Inc., New York.

Library of Congress Cataloging-in-Publication Data is available.
A CIP catalogue record for this book is available from The British Library.
ISBN 0-7358-2017-1 (trade edition)
1 3 5 7 9 10 8 6 4 2
Printed in Belgium

Little Mouse pulled on her blue jacket with pea-green
polka dots.

Standing straight and unmoving on the barnyard fence, her mother watched her go.

Little Mouse looked back to shout good-bye and wave. "Leaving the home where I was born is very hard!" she muttered as she brushed away a tear.

She had never dreamed the world was so big! She walked for a long time down an unfamiliar country road. Sometimes she felt a little afraid. Only a little, though, because she was a very brave mouse.

She passed some clover and buttercups growing along the side of the road. "Do you know of any empty houses around here?" she asked. But the clover chattered among themselves, and the buttercups were too busy glowing in the sun to pay her any attention.

So she turned to a nearby dandelion, who waved
its white head at her.

"Do you know of an abandoned house? I don't
need much, a wee little house would do just fine.
You see, I'm so tired," she added, with a sigh.

It wasn't much of a sigh, a mouse's sigh, just a
slip more than nothing. But that's all it took to
blow away the seeds of that puffy white head,
and there went the dandelion's response.

Little Mouse set off down the road again.

Eventually, she met a snail. She tried to be cheerful.
"Hello! Where are you going?"

"Oh, nowhere," said the snail. "Everything is much too dry.
But when the rain comes, I'll go fast and far."

"Far enough to find a house?" asked Little Mouse.

"Houses don't interest me. I have everything I need. You ought
to carry your house on your back, like snails do. We are always
sure of having a roof over our head."

Two young rabbits got all excited when Little Mouse asked them about a home.

"All the holes around here are taken," said one.

"But you could make yourself a new one!" interrupted the other.

"Just pick a nice woodsy place . . ."

"Then you dig and dig and dig . . ."

"Make lots of rooms, you need lots of rooms and lots of openings . . ."

"Because of the hunters, you know, and the weasels . . ."

"And then you . . ."

Little Mouse somehow couldn't imagine herself digging a hole in the ground. She went on. The two rabbits kept chattering, without stopping to take a breath and didn't even notice that Little Mouse had left.

Little Mouse was afraid there might not be a place for her anywhere.
Then, as the road took a turn, she saw a house—a real house.

Of course, even though it looked nice, it still could hide a thousand dangers. A cat might lurk behind the door, or there could be traps baited with delicious cheese. What if there was a mouse-hungry owl hiding in the attic, just waiting for dark to fall?

Little Mouse decided to risk it.

Inside it was very quiet.

Her whiskers twitched. She didn't smell cat, or cheese in a mousetrap, either. And the house didn't seem to have an attic.

She climbed up onto a table, where, among tubes of paint and white papers, she discovered an even smaller house. It had a pink tiled roof, honeysuckle climbing above the window, and three steps up to the door.

Never had a mouse dreamed of a prettier house!

But it wasn't real. It was just a painting on a piece of paper.

Suddenly Little Mouse heard a noise. She scurried into a jar and hid among some pencils.

A young man came and sat down at the table. "What does a mouse look like?" he groaned. "I just can't get it right!"

Fascinated, Little Mouse pressed her head against the jar, careful not to move any of the pencils.

"How can I illustrate a book about a mouse if I can't draw a good mouse?" the young man said angrily. "If only I had a model to draw from . . ."

Little Mouse felt filled with a sense of purpose. She carefully brushed the pencil shavings from her pants, tugged at her jacket to smooth out the wrinkles, and climbed out of her hiding place as quietly as she could because she didn't want to frighten the young man.

"I would be happy to help you, if you'd like," she said.

It is rare for a young man to be afraid of a mouse. This one roared with laughter.

"You've got a job!" he exclaimed. "Sit there."

Wasting no time, he began to draw. He drew a little mouse in a blue jacket with pea-green polka dots on a country road. He showed her walking and running, and standing near some flowers. Finally, he finished drawing. "You've helped me so much," he said. "What can I do to thank you?"

"Well," replied Little Mouse, "I was looking for a house—like the one in your painting . . ."

"Why, I can make that into a house for you!" the artist said. "With heavy cardboard walls and a well-glued roof!"

"Would it keep out the rain and let in the sun?"

"Yes indeed."

"Would there be cats or owls or mousetraps?"

"It would be too small! They'd never fit inside."

The artist kept his word. And that is how Little Mouse
got a real little house and a place in this book
at the very same time!